The Crystal Flower and the Sun

An Original Persian Folk Story

Story by Faridah Fardjam

Pictures by Nikzad Nojoomi

Translated by Mansoor Alyeshmerni

CAROLRHODA BOOKS

MINNEAPOLIS, MINNESOTA U.S.A.

An Original Persian Folk Story

Copyright © 1972 by CAROLRHODA BOOKS, INC.
241 First Avenue North, Minneapolis, Minnesota.

All rights reserved. Manufactured in the United States of
America. Published simultaneously in Canada by J. M.
Dent and Sons Ltd., Don Mills, Ontario.

Originally published by The Institute for the Intellectual
Development of Children and Young Adults, Tehran, Iran.

International Standard Book Number: 0-87614-017-7
Library of Congress Catalog Card Number: 71-128814

Night filled the sky of the cold arctic circle. The night stayed one month. She stayed two months. She stayed six full months. Then the night began to fall asleep, and the stars blinked out one by one and the moon slowly vanished.

And over faraway lands where painted cities glow in
the dawn, the sun rose into the sky. Then he travelled
and travelled until he reached the cold polar region.

And the orange sun spilled his rays over the land, and ice and snow glistened orange in his light. The sun leaned on the blue wall of the sky and mused to himself, "What a quiet world this is." The air in the sky was cold; the land below him was snow and ice. A lone white bird flew through the air and gleamed in the sun's rays. And time passed.

Then one day faint "chinkle-chinkle" sounds began to come from a small mass of ice far below the sun. Slowly the ice broke open into separate crystal fingers. Gently one finger grew into a tall crystal stem. Clear, pointed pieces of ice pushed themselves out from all around the top of the stem.

One by one, all the colors of the rainbow's silk ribbons appeared in the frozen petals. And there on the ice below the sun stood a crystal flower of sparkling red, orange, yellow, green, deep blue, and violet.

The sun in his journey of a thousand thousand days had seen many flowers—flowers with large petals, flowers with tiny petals. He had seen blue, pink flowers, violet, and white flowers, but he had never before seen a crystal flower.

And the sun spoke to the crystal flower and said, "Crystal flower, you are more lovely than all the flowers that grow in waving green grasses in other lands. There people pick only the loveliest of flowers and place them in vases in rooms. If people were to see you, they would pluck you and put you in a vase in a room. Tell me, how did you come to be?"

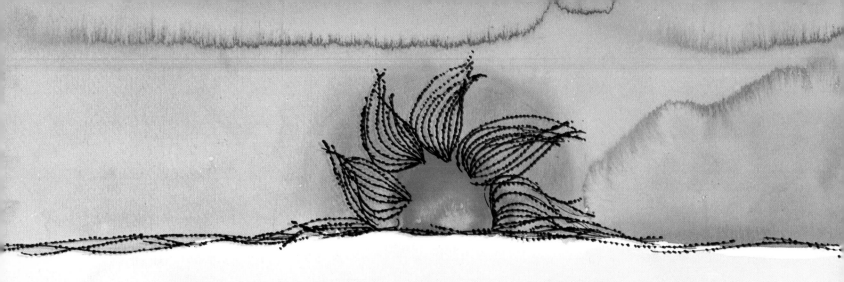

As the crystal flower heard the words of the sun, her rainbow colors sparkled brighter than before, and she said, "I saw your light from behind the ice and followed your rays to come out into the world." Then she asked him, "Sun, how do flowers grow in other lands?"

And the sun answered her, "The flowers pull themselves out of the warm earth and live in my light. All round them the air is fresh. Their stems and leaves bend and flutter in cool breezes."

"Then why," asked the crystal flower, "is my stem stuck to cold ice? Why is it that only wind and snow move around me?"

"Because," said the sun, "here at the north pole nothing lives but wind and cold and snow and ice."

And so they began to talk together, and the sun spoke with the crystal flower for days and days.

And the sun told the crystal flower of all he
had seen in the world. He talked of the cities
and the people in the cities who rush to work.
He told of wondrous things that workers in
factories build. He spoke of lovely houses in
the cities, whose walls glow blue or green,
orange or pink in his rays. And he told her
how he warmed their roofs, their windowpanes,
and their iron gates.

And the sun spoke to the crystal flower of forests so thick that he could not see their floors, of the wheat fields that grow in valleys, of the villagers who work in the fields, and of shepherds' children in woolens of scarlet and brown and green, who tend sheep on green grass hills.

When the sun ended his tales, six months had passed, and the night waited to take his place. The sun began to gather his rays and prepare to leave the cold country. It was time for flowers of other lands to bloom in his warmth and light.

The crystal flower asked, "Sun, why are you gathering up your light?"

And the sun answered, "I must gather up my light little by little and return to the other lands where trees and birds and people are all waiting for the morning."

The crystal flower was sad at the thought of being separated from her friend, and she said, "If you go, the night will come. It will be dark, and I will be able to see nothing and talk with no one."

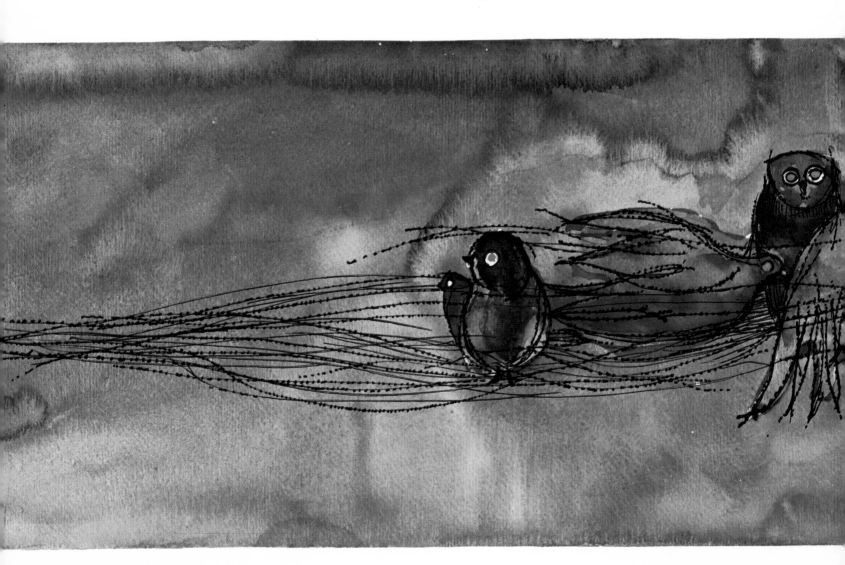

The sun was troubled. He grew dark with worry and rested his head on the dark blue wall of the sky.

Then the sun replied, "You and I have been friends all the six months of light at the pole. But now I must go. Right now, my friends in the cities, fields, and villages are awaiting my return."

The crystal flower cried out, "Sun, Sun, take me with you! Pluck me and put me in a vase in your room. I too want to see greater lands—the cities full of factories and houses, the gardens full of fruits and vegetables and flowers, the fields where people work with the earth, the markets where people laugh and are busy. Take me with you, Sun," pleaded the flower.

But the sun was still troubled and said, "Now you are very far away from me, and all of my heat does not reach you. If you come with me, you will melt. You will no longer be a lovely crystal flower."

But the crystal flower begged to go with him and said, "Even so, I want to go with you to take light to your friends."

So the sun shone and shone his last rays intensely on the crystal flower. And like a golden belt, a shaft of light knotted itself around the stem of the crystal flower and clipped her free of the ice. Then slowly, slowly she rose through the sky, coming closer and closer to her friend.

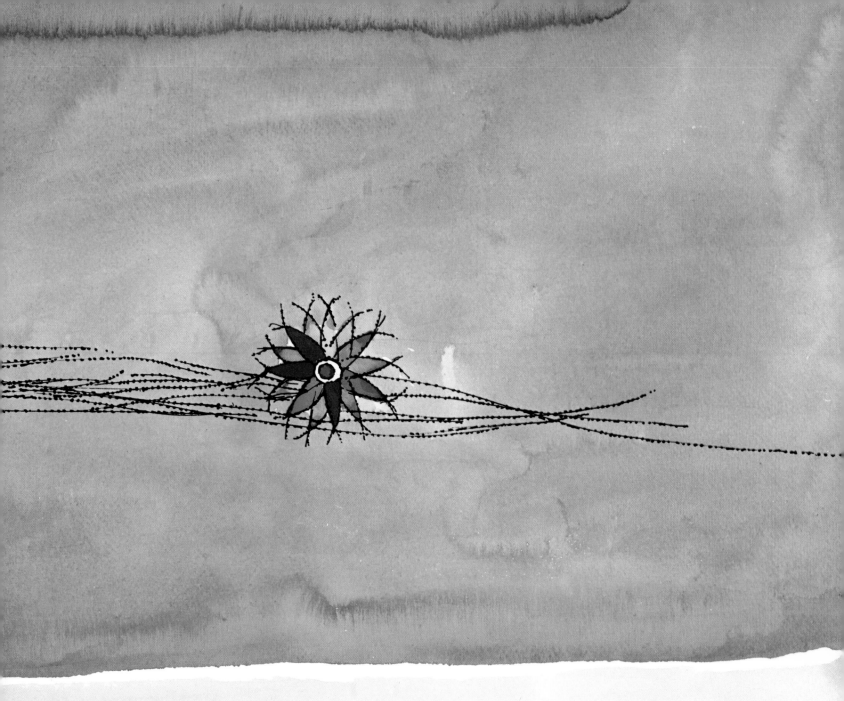

"You are going to melt, lovely flower," sighed the sun.

"It does not matter, for now with you I will bring the morning to the world," replied the flower.

And the sun rolls and rolls over all the world shining his rays of warmth and light. On the face of the sun is a small, dark spot. Some people call it a sunspot. But others know it is really the crystal flower still traveling with the sun.